TALES OF THE TIME DRAGON

DAYS OF THE KNIGHTS

BY ROBERT NEUBECKER

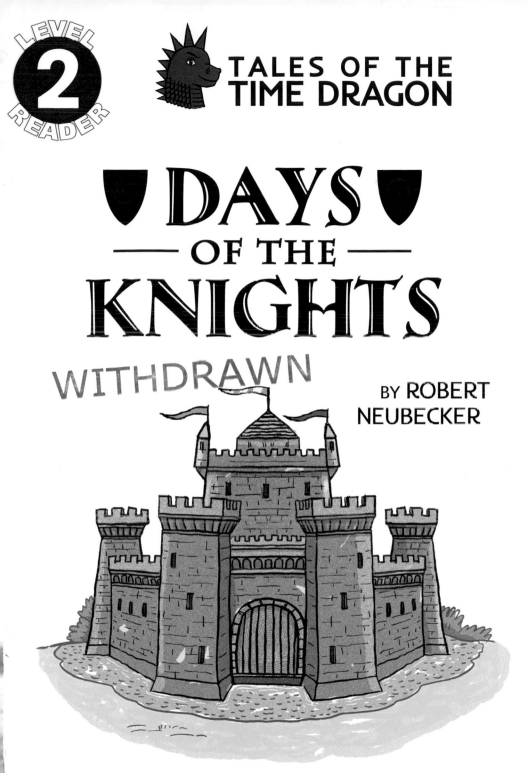

SCHOLASTIC INC.

You are about to travel back in time to the year 1200 and a country called England.

England is a country on the continent of Europe, a whole ocean away from the United States of America.

For Mary Kimball, Cindy Phillips, and educators everywhere.

Library of Congress Cataloging-in-Publication Data
Neubecker, Robert.
Days of the knights / Robert Neubecker.
p. cm. – (Tales of the time dragon ; 1)
Summary: Red the Time Dragon transports Joe and Lilly to England, around 1200 A.D., to teach them about life in the Middle Ages.
ISBN 978-0-545-54898-4 (hardcover)
1. Dragons–Juvenile fiction. 2. Time travel–Juvenile fiction. 3. Middle Ages–Juvenile fiction. 4. Knights and knighthood–Juvenile fiction. 5. England–Civilization–1066-1485–Juvenile fiction. [1. Dragons–Fiction. 2. Time travel–Fiction. 3. Middle Ages–Fiction. 4. Knights and knighthood–Fiction. 5. England–Civilization–1066-1485–Fiction.] I. Title.
PZ7.N4394Day 2014
[E]–dc23
                                    2013007397

12 11 10 9 8 7 6 5 4 3 2 1   14 15 16 17 18 19/0

Printed in South China
First printing, March 2014

"What's up, Joe?" asked Lilly.
"I'm doing a report on the Middle Ages."
Joe shrugged.

"With knights and queens and castles? What fun!"

"I guess so," mumbled Joe.

"I'll help you research," said Lilly. She tapped the keys on the library computer:

M-I-D-D-L-E   A-G-E-S

"Where are we?" Lilly wondered.

"Look!" cried Joe. "Where did that big red dragon come from?"

"Good morning! I'm Red the Time Dragon! I will be your guide to the Middle Ages! It's the year 1200, and we're in England. We have to be careful. Dragons aren't exactly popular here."

"This part of the world has many deep, dark forests filled with wild beasts," said Red. "There are dangers everywhere. Some are real, some are imagined."

"Like dragons," said Lilly.
"Like dragons," agreed Red.
Joe shivered. "Let's get out of here!"

Lilly and Joe climbed onto Red's back. They snuck past a row of houses crowded with people and animals of all kinds.

"Most people are poor here and can't read or write," Red said. "They are called peasants, and they live on farms or in small villages."

"They let cows and pigs inside?" asked Lilly.

"They have to," said Red. "Animals keep them warm on long winter nights. Plus, if you leave your cow outside, someone or something might come along and eat it."

Joe could feel eyes watching them . . . and he wasn't sure they only belonged to the pigs!

The road led to a little town with strong stone walls to keep out strangers.

Shopkeepers watched as they passed by.

"I don't think they like strangers," whispered Joe.
"Yeah," said Lilly. "And what could be stranger than us?"

Soon they came to a harbor. Traders from all over Europe were selling their wares in the marketplace. A long ship rocked gently at the dock.

"Vikings!" said Joe, a bit too loudly.

"Shh!" Red said. "Vikings are great traders and explorers from the north. They bring furs and silk to trade for wool. But they are also fierce warriors!"

Once again, people were staring at them.
Lilly was getting a very bad feeling about the traders in general and the Vikings in particular.

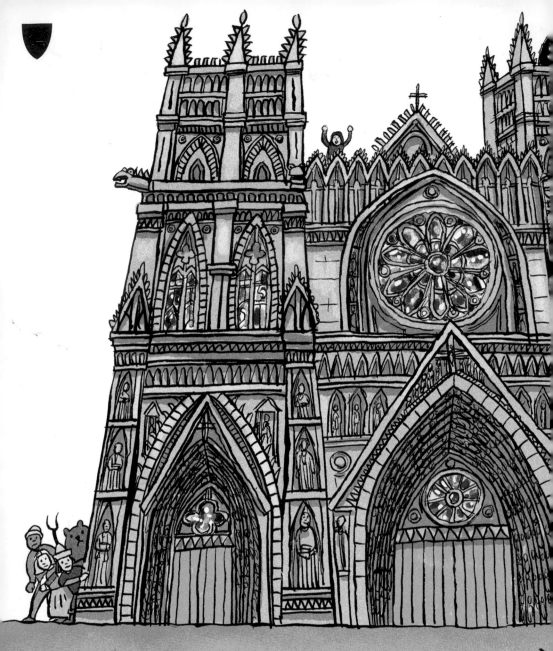

Next, they came upon a huge stone building covered with carvings and beautifully colored windows.

"The great churches are the finest works of art of the Middle Ages," said Red proudly.

"This one must have taken years to build," said Joe.

"Hundreds," Red answered.

Just then, big rocks began to fall from
above. Ugly statues on the tower sprayed
boiling oil. The church bells rang an alarm!
"Time to move on!" Red smiled,
flashing a hundred sharp teeth.
Joe looked over his shoulder.
They were being followed.

"A castle!" Lilly cried.

"A knight named Sir Vile lives here," said Red.
"He owns all the land we've seen. He makes the
peasants pay to use it. And if he were a good
knight, he would protect them in return."

SIR VILE! THE DRAGON!

"But he's a bad one?" asked Lilly.
Red sighed. "Sir Vile takes from them, but gives nothing back. He's a thief and a bully."

"Don't look now, but there's a mob of bullies behind us!" Joe said.

Red turned and faced the crowd.

"I am not the one you should fear," he called. "Who makes you pay to use his land?"

The crowd rumbled. "Sir Vile . . ."

"Who is supposed to protect you?" Red asked.

"Sir Vile."

"Who takes what is yours and gives nothing in return?" Red shouted.

"Sir Vile!"

"Um . . . Red . . . there is a nasty-looking knight heading straight for us!" Joe said.

"And he's got archers!" yelled Lilly. "Duck!"

"Hang on!" said Red gleefully. "Watch this!"

Red breathed fire!

"HOORAY!
HOORAY!"
said the peasants.

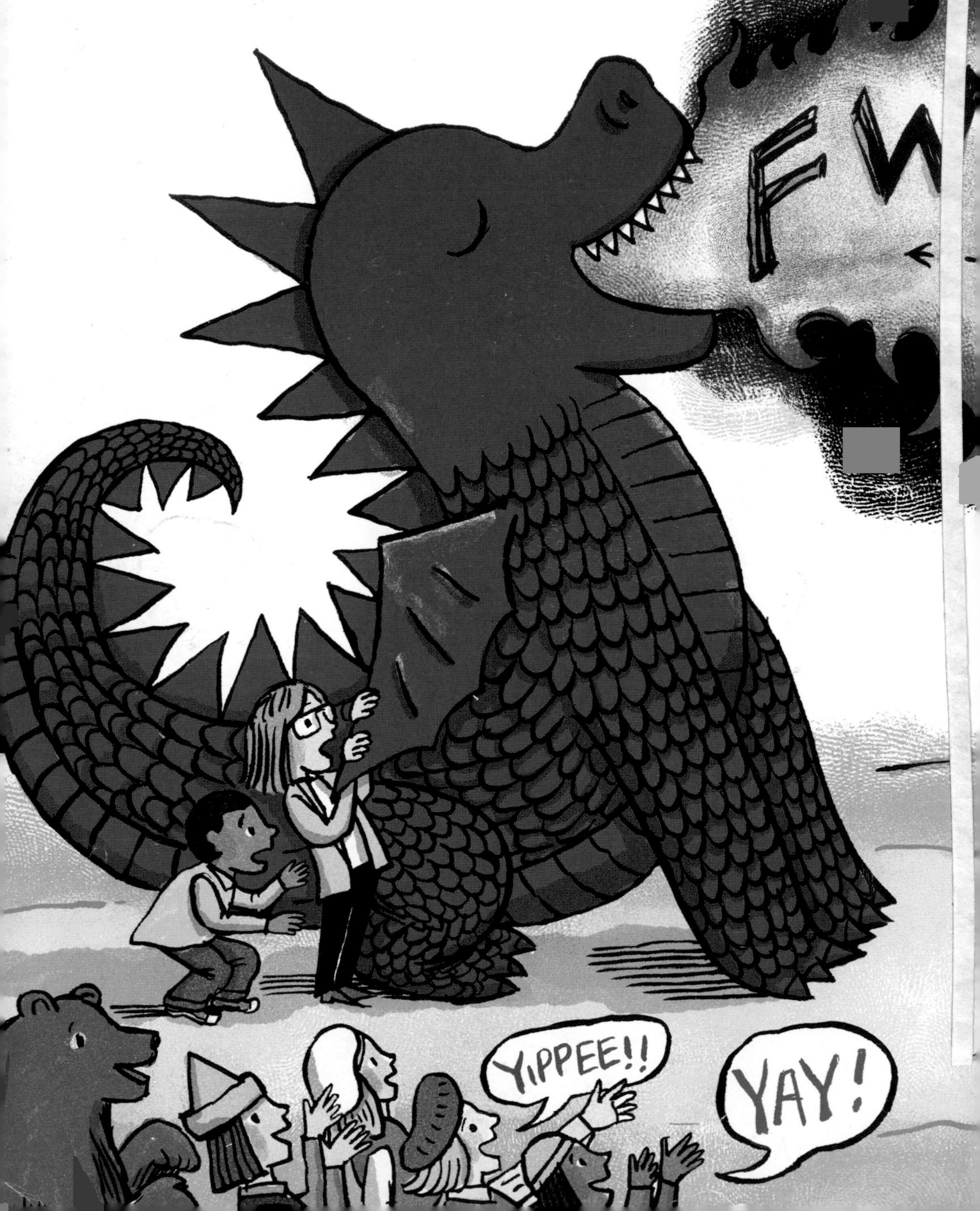

"That was amazing!" said Joe. "And now that you've toasted Sir Vile, how about roasting us some hamburgers?"

"No need," said Lilly. "Look at this feast! Veggies and stew and meat and bread!"

Everyone cheered for Red. They were free of Sir Vile at last.

Joe happily stuffed food into his mouth.

"Joe! Mind your manners!" said Lilly.

"Forks aren't in style," mumbled Joe.

"So, Joe, when is this report due?" asked Red.

"Tomorrow . . ." said Joe.

"Then it's time for you to get back home," said Red.

"Good-bye, Red!" said Lilly and Joe. "Until next time!"

"Um, Lilly, do you have a pencil?" asked Joe.
"Sure!"

Joe started his report. He began by drawing a big red dragon.

More About the Middle Ages

The Middle Ages were a dangerous time. People had to worry about things like having enough to eat, catching a deadly disease, and protecting themselves from wild beasts and outlaws.

At Home

Peasants lived on farms. Their houses had straw roofs and dirt floors. They had to use fire for heat and light. Most people only got a bath twice in their lives: once when they were born and once when they died.

In Town

People who lived in town often owned shops. There were bakers, butchers, and carpenters. Weavers wove cloth. Blacksmiths fixed iron objects like horseshoes. Fletchers made arrows. Chandlers made candles. Barbers cut hair, pulled teeth, and did surgery.

Trade

Traders traveled the world. They bought things like cloth, spices, and furs in one place and sold them in another. Traders faced danger from robbers on the roads and pirates on the sea.

Knights

Knights were mostly rich and lived in castles. They let peasants live on their land. In return, the peasants gave money and some of their crops to the knight.

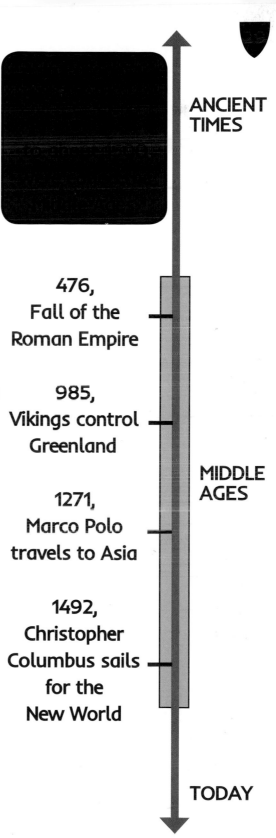

ANCIENT TIMES

476,
Fall of the
Roman Empire

985,
Vikings control
Greenland

1271,
Marco Polo
travels to Asia

MIDDLE AGES

1492,
Christopher
Columbus sails
for the
New World

TODAY

Glossary

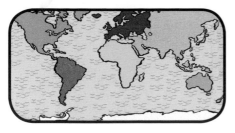

Continent – One of the seven large chunks of land on Earth.

Crops – Plants grown on farms in large amounts.

Empire – A group of countries that have the same ruler.

Knight – A warrior who was given land by a king. In return, the knight would fight—or send soldiers to fight—for the king.

Peasant – A person who worked on a small farm.

Shopkeeper – A person who owned or ran a small shop or store.

Trader – A person who bought and sold things to make money.